The Sugarplum Fairy

SAMANTHA COLE

SUSPENSEFUL SEDUCTION PUBLISHING

One

After climbing into the sleigh, Jasper Sugarplum checked the list on his tablet, then checked it twice, as per the Department of Naughty or Nice Affairs (DNNA) protocols. It was four-and-a-half weeks before Christmas and two days before Thanksgiving, and he'd flown from the North Pole to Wyoming to closely monitor some of the children assigned to him.

He was honored to have one of the most essential positions working for Kris Kringle, or Santa Claus, as most people called him. Jasper's job, along with other agents at DNNA, was to ensure every child around the world was assessed and in the proper category before Santa received the final Naughty & Nice list on Christmas Eve. While Jasper loved what he did, he looked forward to his two-week vacation, which started the moment Santa uttered his yearly spiel—*On Dasher, on Dancer, on Prancer, on Vixen . . .*

Maybe, with a bit of luck, Jasper could find a date for the annual New Year's Eve party at Father Time's to welcome the new baby. The years always went out and came in with a bang, and he wanted to participate in the festivities with a hot guy by his side. The problem was he'd been so busy lately and hadn't been on a date in months—something he wanted to rectify as soon as possible.

Settling onto the well-padded, heated seat, Jasper used the tablet's stylus to mark the appropriate boxes and make several notes about the last few kids he checked in on. "Hector, nice. Emily, nice. Becky, nice. Alberto, improved to nice. And Derek . . . better but still needs a little work."

The latter talked back to his mother earlier and almost earned a naughty mark, but then he apologized so Jasper would give him a second chance. The kid had a few more weeks to get his act together, and hopefully, he would.

As he scanned the names on the ledger once more to make sure he hadn't missed anyone, a strong wind blew through Jasper's hair, and he tilted his head back and sniffed the air. The incoming pre-winter blizzard had cleared the Rockies earlier than expected, and another one was reportedly coming in right behind the first. The North Pole Weather Bureau had posted warnings over the past forty-eight hours, but Jasper thought he'd be done with his cases before the first storm hit. Now, it looked like it would be a bumpy ride until he and his reindeer got further north.

After tucking his DNNA tablet into his canvas bag, he put it in the compartment under his seat for safekeeping. He then picked up the reins, letting Nip, the temporary reindeer assigned to him, know it was time to get moving. His regular sidekick, Digger, injured his hoof the other day during the weekly reindeer games that kept the teams in shape. The NP veterinarian put him on the injured reserve list for at least a week, so Jasper had to make do with the temp. He just wished Nip had more experience flying through bad weather —this was only the third time he'd seen any action since being approved for intercontinental flights a month ago. He and Jasper's first two trips had gone off without a hitch, with clear skies and no rough air currents. Hopefully, they'd make it over the Canadian border before things got too bad tonight.

As if Mother Nature heard his thoughts, snow began to fall, and not just light flurries, but thick, heavy flakes that swirled around the sleigh.

Great. Just great.

He pulled his wool hat down over his pointed ears and slid his hands into a pair of fleece-lined gloves. He retrieved a pair of goggles from a storage compartment under the seat and put them on. As soon as they hit cruising altitude, it would be negative fifty degrees Fahrenheit, but the windchill would drop the number even further. However, that was par for the course this time of year, and Jasper was used to it.

Bracing himself for liftoff, he tugged at the reins. "Ready to go, Nip?"

When the antlered animal turned his head and nodded, Jasper gave him a thumbs-up. "Awesome. Let's head home and then grab us some brandy and snicker-doodles." That was his favorite post-flight treat, and he could almost taste the cinnamon sugar cookies and amber liquor waiting for him. "Onward, Nip!"

The reindeer took off at a gallop, and within six seconds, his hooves no longer hit the ground. He became airborne with the sleigh trailing behind him, lifting just in time for both to clear some pine trees. They climbed higher and higher as the snow grew heavier. Less than five minutes later, they were in near whiteout conditions, but between the sleigh's GPS and radar guidance system, Jasper didn't expect to run into any problems.

When they leveled off, he sighed in relief. Takeoffs and landings were the worst in harsh weather, and Jasper's stomach always tended to drop during those times. As they cruised along, he kept his eyes on the radar. So far, Nip was doing well. Jasper would give him high marks on the Reindeer Evaluation Sheet, which he needed to fill out when they got home. While he only had to do that for Digger if there was a flight incident, for the probationary reindeer, it was a requirement.

A quick check of the GPS told him they had just flown over the Wyoming/Montana border and were south of Bozeman and west of Custer Gallatin National Forest. On nights like this, he wished all the reindeer had Rudolph's shiny red nose to break through the darkness and the warp-speed appearance of the snow.

The wind picked up even more, and the sleigh rocked hard as they flew through a patch of turbulence. Jasper's grip on the reins tightened. It was a doozy of a storm, and he silently cursed himself for staying out longer than he should have. Nip was having difficulty remaining steady as he battled the elements. While they could attempt to get above the blizzard, the lower oxygen levels wouldn't allow them to stay there long.

Jasper debated whether to climb higher, even just for a few minutes, to see if they could escape the worst part of the storm. But before he could come to a decision, Nip and the sleigh were hit hard by a gust of wind that tilted them both to the side. Jasper wasn't ready for sudden motion and slid across the seat. He was about to grab onto the railing in front of him, but another pocket of uneven air rocked the sleigh, and suddenly, Jasper was airborne—by himself.

At first, he panicked, as gravity caused him to plummet toward the earth at a high rate of speed. He spun, twirled, and flipped to the point he didn't know which way was up. But then his training took over, and he felt for the cord at his hip. When his fingers found it, he yanked on it, and his safety parachute deployed, slowing his descent.

With his heart pounding, Jasper knew he wasn't out of the woods yet. The violent winds jerked him in one direction and then another. In the darkness, he had no idea what was below him or how long he had before landing. Holding onto the straps of the parachute, he tried to keep the canopy from twisting and becoming useless. Once he was no longer flying through the air, with the not-so-greatest of ease, he would activate his tracking beacon, letting the North Pole know he was in trouble and needed them to send out a rescue team. But first, he had to get his feet on solid ground.

Myriad trees appeared below his feet a second before he started hitting them. Pine needle-covered branches swatted his limbs, torso, and face before he was jerked to a stop. Breathing heavily, he looked up to see the parachute was caught on the top of a spectacular Douglas fir, leaving him hanging high above the forest floor. A glance downward had his stomach roiling.

Well, reindeer crap.

He was about sixty feet in the air—too far to just let himself drop, and the parachute couldn't free itself with his weight pulling it down.

As he swayed amidst the storm, he eyed the tree he was in. While he was about ten feet from the top of the massive thing, the trunk and boughs appeared strong enough to support his weight for brief periods. He needed to get the parachute straps off to start the treacherous climb down to the ground. Thank goodness all this was part of his training—but never in the middle of a freaking blizzard, thank you very much.

Taking advantage of his body's pendulum motion, he rocked harder until he could wrap his legs around the tree trunk. Grabbing a limb, he pulled himself closer to the tree's center. Once confident he had a good grip and the tree would hold him, Jasper found the multi-purpose tool attached to his belt and used the knife attachment to cut through the straps around his torso and over his shoulders. As soon as he was free, without his weight holding it down, the parachute ripped from the top of the tree and flew away.

Taking a deep breath, Jasper let it out, then slowly began to work his way down the tree. His feet slipped occasionally, and several times, he was tempted to remove his gloves to get a better grip, but he knew their thickness protected his hands. With the heavy snow still coming down, it was difficult to see where the next branch was to put his feet on. At one point, about a third of the way down, his jacket caught on a sharp twig, and as he tried to maneuver himself free, he heard the fabric tear. Before he realized what was happening, his tracking beacon was ripped off his jacket and hurtled to the ground, disappearing into a pile of snow.

Cookie cutters!

Hopefully, the device hadn't been damaged in the fall.

Jasper eyed the distance he still had to go—twenty, maybe twenty-five feet. An estimated eight or nine inches of snow blanketed the forest bed—four of which fell the night before. It was still coming down like crazy, and from the forecast, they expected close to a foot and a half before the storm was over.

As he looked for the next branch he could step on, another strong gust of wind blew through the trees, and the bough Jasper's right foot balanced on snapped under his weight. There was no chance to catch himself before he plunged toward the earth, bouncing off the rest of the branches, each one more painful than the last. He landed on the ground with a resounding thud, and the breath was knocked from his lungs. Agony briefly coursed through his body before it faded as his mind went black.

Two

Mack Wynters dropped his spoon into the now-empty soup bowl in front of him and grabbed a napkin to wipe his mouth. The New England clam chowder he cooked for dinner hit the spot as he relaxed at the dining table in his beautiful secluded chalet while the blizzard outside kicked up a notch. The eight-room structure had been his refuge from the rest of the world for the past three-and-a-half years, even more so during the holiday seasons, which were fast approaching once again.

Thanksgiving he could deal with, as he and Baxter would spend the day together watching the college football games and enjoying an assorted spread like Mack's mother used to put out for their extended family to enjoy. Of course, he and the one-hundred-sixty-pound St. Bernard didn't need as much food as Jessica Wynters had prepared for fifteen to twenty people each year—but it was close. Mack and Baxter didn't bother with the turkey and fixings either—that was too much food on top of all the snacks they planned to enjoy.

What destroyed him each year, though, was a different holiday. It was the fact he had to deal with all things Christmas, starting just after Halloween. The advertisements, the movies, the TV shows, the decorations all over town, the Santa Claus at the mall, the jingle bells, the music . . . shit, the music was the freaking worst. And people walking around with holiday cheer, wishing everyone they saw a "Merry Christmas."

Bah-humbug.

Every year for the past three, it was nothing but torture for eight-plus weeks.

Earlier in the week, as soon as he learned about the possibility of a heavy snowstorm, followed closely by a second one, he made the dreaded trip into town to stock up on food and essentials and fill up the spare gas tanks for his generator. The latter would be used for the water heater, the refrigerator, and a chest freezer he kept in the garage.

If the power went out, Mack didn't need to worry about the lack of heat or lights. More than enough firewood was stacked up behind the house to make it through even the worst of winters. A potbelly stove sat in each of the three bedrooms, while a large stone fireplace was the focal point in the great room, which was a living room, dining room, and study combined. The well-insulated chalet's open floor plan would also keep the kitchen nice and warm. For lighting, many windows in each room let the sun shine in during the daytime. At night, candles and battery-operated lanterns would do. In the past, many a night, he typed away on a new novel by candlelight. While everything eventually ended up on his computer, he sometimes enjoyed writing on an old manual typewriter. It'd been a present from Michael—one he treasured more than any other.

Mack sighed as his fiancé filled his thoughts, which happened often, even after all this time. Michael Sherman was the reason Mack had loved Christmas and then hated it. They met through mutual friends eight years ago and immediately hit it off. Twelve months later, they moved in together, followed by getting engaged another two-and-a-half years after that.

Michael, a high school teacher, had loved every holiday, from the obvious to the obscure, and decorated their home and his classroom for each one. But Christmas had been his favorite. Every year, he went all out, adding new things to the vast display in the front yard of the home they shared in the suburbs of Manchester. For weeks, dozens of people would drive by every night to look at it.

The decorations inside the house had been even more elaborate. Those who attended their annual holiday party each year marveled at how beautiful it all looked. And even though Mack grumbled about having to unpack everything and put it up two weeks before Thanksgiving—yup, Michael had insisted—and then take it all down again after New Year's, he secretly enjoyed it.

But all that came to a screeching halt one afternoon almost three years ago. While preparing for a small gathering of friends on Christmas Eve, Michael realized they were running low on eggnog. Mack was stacking wood next to their fireplace and offered to run to the store, but his fiancé had already grabbed his keys and coat, heading for the door. An hour later, after Mack left two voicemail messages and sent three texts, there was a knock at the door. He would never forget the solemn faces of the two police officers standing on his front porch. He could still hear their words of regret as they told him the love of his life was stolen from him at the hands of a driver who had too much holiday cheer and ran a stoplight. Mack's world crumbled that day, and he'd never recovered.

Thanks to family and friends, all the decorations had been put away. When Mack sold the house a few months later, because he couldn't stand living there with all the memories of Michael in each room, he left all the boxes of holiday decorations for the new owners. He only kept a beautiful gold Christmas ornament that had been in Michael's family for generations. Michael insisted it was the first one hung on the tree each year. If it hadn't been a treasured family heirloom, Mack would've left it with all the other stuff he gave away.

Once Mack permanently moved to the chalet he and Michael bought as a vacation home in Blunt, Montana, he buried himself in his writing, much to his publisher's delight. He poured his anger, loathing, and grief into each line of every chapter. The result was thirteen books in three years, each reaching the top ten on all the bestseller lists. Four novels had been turned into screenplays, with two already filmed. The first was scheduled to be released next spring, and he was already fighting with his agent about attending the premiere. Fame and fortune were not what Mack wanted. Yes, the money was handy when it came time to pay the bills, but he didn't want to be surrounded by people asking him personal questions and wanting him to smile for photos. All he wanted was to be alone, with Baxter, and write.

Each year, his friends and family invited him for the holidays, and each year, he turned them down. While his parents both passed away years ago, his brother and sister still tried to reach out to him. Scott and Julie said they understood his reasoning for being a recluse, but he doubted they really did. He knew he hurt them by staying away, but the last thing he wanted was to put on a fake smile for everyone else's sake.

Getting to his feet, Mack picked up his bowl and started for the kitchen. Before he reached the threshold, Baxter growled at the front door. While the snow had eased a bit for the moment, the wind picked up again and battered the sides of the house. The dog often heard animals scurrying around outside, but he rarely reacted aside from lifting his ears to listen for a threat.

When Baxter let out a few loud barks, Mack's eyes narrowed at him. "What is it, boy?"

He wondered what the dog had heard. It was doubtful any large animals, like moose or wildcats, would roam around in this kind of weather. They were probably hunkered down under any available shelter through the worst of the storm.

When another round of barking ensued, accompanied by the dog scratching at the front door, Mack walked over to him. "Something outside?"

He opened the door to check, knowing Baxter was wise enough not to engage any animal larger than him. The St. Bernard ran outside, sniffing the air. He then circled back to the porch and woofed at Mack before making a beeline to the trees to the west. Before disappearing into the forest, the dog stopped and turned back to his owner, barking to get his attention. It was evident Baxter wanted Mack to follow him.

The last time he'd done that was back in September. When Mack finally figured out what the dog wanted and trailed after him for a half mile, it was to find an injured bald eagle struggling to fly with an arrow through its wing. With the aid of a Montana game warden, the majestic bird was brought to a local rescue, where it was currently rehabilitating until it could be returned to the wild. Unfortunately, whoever illegally shot it hadn't been caught yet.

Wondering what kind of animal Baxter wanted him to help this time, Mack shook his head as he fetched a heavy coat from the hall closet and pulled on a pair of snow boots. A hat, gloves, and scarf went on next. In case he ran into an aggressive moose, Mack retrieved the rifle that hung over the fireplace and made sure he had extra ammo in his pockets. The last thing he grabbed was his grandfather's compass from a side table drawer in the living room. If they ended up in a whiteout, he would need it to find his way back to the house, although Baxter usually had a great sense of direction no matter the weather.

Shutting the door behind him, Mack cursed the frigid biting wind as he trudged after Baxter, dancing at the edge of the forest, barking and telling his human to get a move on. "All right, dog. This better be important because it's colder than a witch's tit out here."

It was a good ten minutes of fighting the elements before man and beast came to a stop. While under the canopy of trees, the snow wasn't as heavy where they stood. However, seven or eight inches covered the ground. Mack's eyes widened as Baxter nosed and pawed at someone lying in the snow. As he hurried over, Mack could see it was an unconscious man wearing a bright red coat, a red-and-white hat with a matching scarf, black gloves, and black boots. He looked to be in his mid-thirties, but that's all Mack could tell.

Glancing around, he frowned, looking for any sign of a snowmobile, an ATV, or skis—but nothing was in sight. Hell, there weren't even any footprints. What in the world was the man doing outside in the middle of a damn blizzard? And how had he gotten there?

Mack pushed aside his curiosity and removed a glove to feel for a pulse. The man's body was still warm under the scarf, and thankfully, his carotid throbbed under Mack's fingers. His chest also rose and fell steadily with each breath he took. He couldn't have been there long because his lips weren't blue with hypothermia, but that could change in a heartbeat.

After setting his rifle down against a tree, Mack grasped the other man's arm, pulled him up, and threw him over his shoulder in a fireman's carry. Thank fuck Mack kept up his cardio and weight training. Whenever he needed to think about where a scene in his current work-in-progress would go next, he'd head into his home gym or go outside to chop some more wood for the winter months. All that work came in handy right then. While the man was smaller than Mack's six-foot-three, two-hundred-twenty-pound frame, he was still heavy enough to make the journey back home in the snow a difficult one.

Once Mack was sure the man was secure on his shoulder, he retrieved his rifle. Even with Baxter in the lead and most of their footprints still visible from the trek out, it took them about twenty-five minutes to get back to the house. Under his clothing, Mack sweated from the exertion as he climbed the stairs to the front porch and opened the door. He strode past the living room and brought the unresponsive man into the only spare bedroom that had an actual bed. He'd brought it from the old house just to get it out of there, but it hadn't been used since. In fact, it still had the clean sheets his sister put on it after his family helped him move in. The comforter was dusty, but he could use clean blankets from the hall closet.

After yanking the top cover from the bed and tossing it to the floor, Mack laid the man down on the mattress and the crisp white bedsheets. He couldn't get an ambulance or rescue unit this far up the mountain during the storm, so he'd have to make him comfortable until it ended and the roads were clear. That could take a few days. Hopefully, the guy wasn't badly hurt or ill because Mack's first aid training was limited from long ago when he was a lifeguard in his teens.

The first thing he knew he had to do was strip off the man's wet clothing and warm him up. The potbelly stove in the corner of the room was empty, but the flue was cleaned three months ago when he had the chimney sweep guys in to prepare for the colder weather.

He whistled softly for Baxter. When the dog appeared in the doorway, Mack said, "Bax, firewood."

As ordered, the dog trotted off to do his job. The first year Mack lived there, the dog watched him cut and stack the firewood, then carry the loads into the house. Baxter soon took it upon himself to help by picking up a piece in his mouth, following his owner inside, and dropping it by the fireplace. It wasn't long before Mack could tell the St. Bernard to retrieve some wood, and the darn dog would do it.

Turning back to his patient, Mack hoped the guy wouldn't be embarrassed when he woke up and found himself stripped, but it was necessary under those conditions. Starting with the boots, Mack worked carefully to get the man undressed. The flannel-lined pants and shirt he found under the heavy winter jacket could've explained why the man still didn't look hypothermic. Right? Again, Mack didn't think the other man had been exposed to the elements long before he was discovered. And that brought back the questions of what he'd been doing out there in the first place and how he'd gotten there.

Gently rolling the man back and forth, Mack managed to get him out of his clothing, leaving only a pair of bright red boxer briefs on him—an interesting color. As he looked for injuries, finding none on the man's front torso, arms, and legs, Mack couldn't help but admire the pale yet toned body stretched out before him. It was ages since he'd gotten aroused and hard, and damn it, now was not the time for that to happen.

Not with an unconscious stranger.

Tearing his gaze away, Mack went to the hall closet and returned with several blankets, spreading each one on top of the prone man. Once he was covered with multiple layers, Mack realized his patient still wore the red-and-white knit cap and reached up to remove it. When he tugged the material free, shoulder-length blond hair stuck out in all directions from static electricity. But that's not what snagged Mack's attention. What he saw had his eyes narrowing.

"What the—"

Three

Gently grabbing the man's chin, Mack turned his head to the side to get a better look at his ears.

Unfreakingbelievable!

What would people think of next? Piercings and tattoos, he understood. Ear gauging, he couldn't quite wrap his head around—it was a fad he hoped would die out. But this? This was weirder than anything he'd ever seen someone do to their body. Somehow, the guy had altered the tops of his ears, so they were . . . *pointy*, like fairies, Spock from *Star Trek*, or Christmas elves.

Bending down to take a closer look, Mack tried to determine if they resulted from some surgical procedure or if they were fake and glued on. He couldn't see any scars or glued edges on the front of the ears, and he didn't want to inspect them too closely while the man was out like a light. Mack straightened and shook his head.

Whatever.

When Baxter trotted in with a third piece of wood, Mack met him by the stove. The dog dropped his cargo unceremoniously by the first two he'd brought in. Mack smirked at him. "The next thing you gotta learn is how to stack them neatly, but that'll do. I still need a few more, though. Go on, Baxter, firewood."

As the dog rushed out to do his master's bidding, Mack opened the cast iron door and began loading up the stove. A few minutes later, he had a nice fire going and joined Baxter in fetching more wood.

Returning to his patient, Mack gently felt around the back of the man's head and found a nice-sized lump under the soft blond hair. It wasn't bleeding, and he tried to remember whether that was good or bad. He then carefully rolled the man onto his side and inspected his back. There was some mild bruising on one shoulder blade, his left tricep, both hips, and his right thigh. Had he fallen onto his back? But how? From the tree he was found under?

Confused, with no answers to his unspoken questions, Mack made the man as comfortable as possible, then adjusted the blankets again so he was completely under them except for his head.

Since there was nothing else he could do until the storm let up and he could call for an ambulance or the man woke up, Mack strode to the door but then hesitated. He glanced back at the bed. Maybe he shouldn't leave him alone in there. What if he vomited from a concussion or something? Or freaked out when he came to in a strange place?

Decision made, Mack left the room but was back a short time later with two bottles of water, one of which he set on the nightstand next to the bed, his reading glasses, a ballpoint pen, and the notebook he currently used to plot out his next book. Settling on a comfortable, upholstered chair and ottoman in the corner of the room, Mack eyed the stranger for a few minutes. Was he a local? Mack didn't go into town often—only when he was low on supplies—so even if the man in his bed were from around there, he wouldn't have recognized him.

Mack studied the man's face and wondered what color eyes he had. Even in his current condition, the guy was handsome. High cheekbones, an elegantly straight nose, a firm jaw, and full lips all made quite a striking impression. What would it be like to kiss that bow-shaped mouth?

He huffed in disgust at where his thoughts had gone, then glanced at Baxter lying on the rug next to the ottoman, staring at him. "What're you looking at?"

The dog's only response was a tilt of his head. Mack rolled his eyes. "Never mind. I've got work to do."

After one more quick glance at the attractive stranger, Mack clicked his pen and set the tip on the first clean page of the notebook.

Four

Jasper awoke with a pounding headache. Every inch of his body hurt, especially his back. It took a Herculean effort to raise his eyelids. When the darkened room came into focus, he glanced around without moving his head.

Where the heck am I?

Wherever he was, it definitely wasn't the North Pole. Instead, it was a warm, comfortable bedroom he didn't recognize. The last thing he remembered was being in his sleigh as he and Nip battled the storm on their way back home, and then he somehow ended up in a tree. After that, there was a whole lot of nothing in terms of memories.

Closing his eyes again, he tried to contact North Pole Mission Control (NPMC) via telepathy but couldn't get through. He reached back and winced when he found a snowball-sized hematoma on his head. Well, that would explain things being out of whack—it would probably take a day or two for his brain transmissions to reset and come back online.

Since he couldn't get in touch with NPMC that way, hopefully, they'd find him through his tracking beacon, although he couldn't remember if he had activated it yet. Regardless, when Nip and the empty sleigh returned without him, a missing elf alert would go out, and everyone would do what they could to locate him. But first things first, he had to figure out where he was.

Pushing up on his elbows, he tried to get a better look at his surroundings. A blue nightlight plugged into an outlet gave off just enough glow so he could see the rest of the room. He was lying on a queen-sized bed opposite a dresser and next to a nightstand. On his right was a set of sliding doors to what he assumed was a closet. On his other side was a potbelly stove in one corner and a chair and ottoman in the other. And sitting on the chair with his legs up was a large man with his arms crossed and his eyes closed, snoring.

Before Jasper could process that, a colossal blurry mass jumping onto the bed beside him almost had him yelling out loud, but then he realized it was a friendly St. Bernard coming to check on him. He didn't have to worry about it attacking him because all animals responded to elves in the same manner—with respect and affection. Even the most ferocious beasts on the planet bowed down to the semi-immortals who were part of Santa's alliance. While elves appeared and sounded like humans, they far outlived their counterparts. In fact, Jasper was 320 years old and looked damn fine for his age if you asked him.

Lifting a hand, he stroked the dog's thick fur and spoke in a low voice so as not to wake the man across the room. "Hey, there. What's your name?"

Being fluent in both canine and feline, Jasper was able to translate the dog's soft woofs. "Taliesin the Snow Hunter. But my master calls me Baxter. I'll respond to both."

"Good to know. Since I don't want to explain to your master why I'm calling you Taliesin, I'll call you Baxter if that is okay with you."

With a little yap, the dog gave his consent.

Over in the corner, the man shifted in the chair but didn't wake up, which gave Jasper a chance to study him. Big and burly was the first thing that came to his mind, with sexy as sin a close second. He looked to be about thirty-five. His broad shoulders, massive chest, and muscular arms had Jasper's hands itching to touch them. The short, honey-brown hair on his head matched the beard and mustache gracing his jaw and upper lip. His long legs and torso had Jasper guessing he stood over six feet tall, several inches above Jasper's own five feet nine inches. Contrary to popular belief, not all elves were little people.

Turning back to the dog, Jasper asked, "Where am I, and how did I get here?"

Long story short, he fell out of the tree and was

knocked unconscious. Baxter and his master rescued Jasper and brought him back home. Okay, that explained a few things but didn't help with his current crisis. He'd been in a few pickles before, but nothing he couldn't handle. This time, with the storm still raging outside and no way to contact NPMC directly, he would have to fabricate a story for Baxter's master until a team could be sent to retrieve him. Hopefully, that would happen before he had to explain to the man why his injuries disappeared within twenty-four hours. Healing at a faster rate was another difference between elves and humans.

He shook the dog's paw. "Thank you for saving me."

Baxter licked his hand in response.

Taking a deep breath, Jasper was about to catalog his injuries when he suddenly realized he was naked under the covers.

What the—?

Lifting the blankets, he ran his hand down his torso, relieved to find he was still wearing his briefs. Okay, so not completely naked. But the knowledge that his human rescuer had stripped him of most of his clothing was actually a turn-on instead of an embarrassment. He could almost feel the man's hands caressing his skin, and that had him hardening.

Reindeer crap! This is not the time to get freaking horny, you idiot. Think!

Right. Okay. Think, think, think. Come up with a believable story for why you were found unconscious in the middle of nowhere. Something that won't sound strange to your rescuer, like you're an elf who fell out of a sleigh on your way back to the North Pole.

Jasper's hands flew to his ears.

Jumpin' jingle bells!

His hat was gone. Had the man seen his elfin ears? Hopefully, he hadn't noticed. Running his fingertips over the points, Jasper transformed them into human-looking ears. That talent came in handy when elves needed to blend in with the rest of the world's population. Unfortunately, the magic would reverse itself when Jasper's defenses were down, like when he was sleeping, sick, or having sex.

You have more important things to deal with right now, so stop thinking about sex!

Oops, he must have said that out loud because Baxter's head tilted, and his eyes widened a bit. Before Jasper could apologize to the animal, he felt another set of eyes on him. Those were more intense than the canine ones.

"You're awake." The man's deep, rumbling voice skated across Jasper's skin, causing goose bumps and sending his blood rushing south. All he could do as the handsome man stood, moved closer, and loomed over him was nod.

"I'm Mack Wynters." He gestured toward the dog still lying next to Jasper. "Baxter found you unconscious in the woods, and I brought you back to my house. Unfortunately, with the storm, I couldn't call for an ambulance or drive you down the mountain to the hospital. How're you feeling?"

"I . . . um . . . I'm okay, I guess. A little banged up but nothing that won't heal." That was true, just much faster than the other man realized.

"Good. That's good." He turned on the bedside lamp, and the soft light illuminated the room. Shoving his hands into the front pockets of his sweatpants, Mack paused as if waiting for the stranger in his bed to say more, but when nothing was forthcoming, he asked, "Um, what's your name?"

Duh. When someone introduced themselves, the polite thing was to do the same, but Jasper had been too distracted by his mountain man's commanding presence.

Holy peppermint, he's even more gorgeous awake.

Damn it! Concentrate!

"Uh, Jasper —" He cleared his suddenly dry throat. "My name's Jasper Sugarplum, but my friends call me Jazz."

Mack's eyebrows shot up, almost to his hairline. "Jasper *Sugarplum*? That's a . . . um . . . an unusual name."

Jasper pursed his lips and shrugged. "Yeah, well, that's what happens when you have unusual parents." And this guy didn't even know the half of it. "So, um, where—where are we? I mean, I know we're in your house, but where's that?"

"You don't know where you were before you got

hurt?" Jasper was about to make up something when Mack's eyes narrowed, and his gaze flittered back and forth to either side of the elf's face. "What happened to your ears?"

Oh, figgy pudding! He did notice them!

Thinking fast, Jasper tried to act confused by the question. "My ears? What do you mean? What's wrong with my ears?"

"They were . . ." A perplexed expression crossed Mack's face, and then he ran his finger over his own ear. "Weren't they, um . . . pointy?"

Five

J asper reached up and ran his fingers through his blond hair, which resulted in it covering the tips of his ears. "Uh, not that I know of."

Now Mack felt like an idiot. He must have been dreaming or hallucinating earlier because, clearly, the other man's ears looked just like his. It was time to change the subject. "Are you hungry? I have some clam chowder I could heat up for you."

A growling stomach followed by an adorable blush were his responses, and Mack chuckled. "I'll take that as a yes. Stay here—I don't want you getting dizzy with that knot on your head. I'll heat up a bowl and bring it in."

"Thank you. I haven't eaten since breakfast, so I could eat an entire gingerbread village right now." When Mack's brow furrowed at the odd statement, Jasper quickly added, "But chowder sounds great."

As the other man lay back down, Mack couldn't help but let his gaze roam over Jasper's naked chest and abs. The covers had fallen to his waist when he sat up, and he didn't appear to be in a rush to pull them back over himself again. Forcing his gaze to Jasper's face, Mack was surprised to see heat and lust there. In fact, the guy was eye-fucking Mack, whose body started to respond.

Shit.

The guy was an absolute stranger, yet all Mack wanted to do was climb onto the bed and fuck him senseless. Mack's breath caught as his mind filled with all the naughty things he suddenly wanted to do with Jasper. Never had he experienced such an instant, visceral attraction like that to someone he'd just met, other than Michael, but, holy hell, was it powerful. It made him want to reach out and yank the covers the rest of the way off Jasper's body so he could see if the guy was as hard as he was.

Shaking the dirty thoughts from his head, Mack spun on his heel and strode out the door, finally exhaling a breath he'd held. Glancing down, he cursed himself. Jasper couldn't have missed Mack's prominent erection. His gray sweatpants didn't do a thing to hide it.

In the kitchen, he turned on the faucet, then ran cold water over his wrists and hands before splashing some on his face. Now was not the time for his long-absent libido to decide to wake up. Once his body was under control, Mack reheated a bowl of the clam chowder and prepared a tray with a glass of ginger ale, some saltines, a napkin, and a soup spoon.

As the microwave plate spun around, Mack heard the hallway bathroom door shut. He hoped Jasper didn't get dizzy and listened carefully for any signs of trouble. A few moments later, the toilet flushed, and the door reopened. Good.

When the microwave dinged, Mack added the heated bowl to the tray and carried it into the spare bedroom. Jasper was back in bed, sitting up, and leaning against the headboard. "That smells delicious," he said as Mack set the tray over his lap. "Thank you."

"Start on that while I get you some ibuprofen. You have a lot of bruises on your back and a lump on your head. You have to be hurting." He wanted to ask how Jasper had gotten injured, but as the man dug into his meal, Mack decided it could wait a little longer. Jasper still hadn't answered Mack's earlier questions yet about what he was doing in the woods or how he'd gotten there in the first place.

Ten minutes later, Jasper had been fed both food and a couple of ibuprofen caplets, and Mack took the tray back to the kitchen. During his patient's meal, they'd made small talk about the weather, but now it was time for Mack to push for answers to his other questions. Returning to the spare bedroom, he sighed when he found Jasper asleep again and Baxter nuzzled against the man's side. Mack quietly stepped over and pulled the covers up over the naked torso he wanted to inspect further with his fingers and tongue. Otherwise, he might give in to the temptation to kick Baxter out of the bed and take the dog's spot.

Turning off the bedside lamp, Mack used the glow from the nightlight to check on the stove. After throwing a few more pieces of wood inside, he closed the iron door and then returned to his chair. Getting comfortable again, Mack studied Jasper's face until he felt his eyes grow heavy. As sleep pulled him under, pointy-eared sugarplum fairies danced in his head.

Six

Yawning, Jasper stretched, grateful he wasn't as sore as last night. His injuries were healing and would be completely gone by the end of the day. Hopefully, NPMC would be able to locate him, send a team, and have him out of there before his sexy-as-mistletoe rescuer noticed Jasper was . . . different than anyone else he'd ever met.

Speaking of his rescuer, Mack no longer sat on the chair in the corner of the room. According to his internal alarm clock, it was just after 8:00 a.m., and Jasper couldn't remember the last time he slept so late. Climbing from bed, he stepped over to the window between the chair and stove, separated two blinds, and peeked out.

"Cookie cutters," he cursed under his breath. The snow still came down at a rate of over an inch per hour, and the wind slammed some severe gusts against the house.

Closing his eyes, Jasper focused on contacting NPMC, but again, he was met with silence from the Arctic Circle. He glanced around the room, searching for his clothing, but it was nowhere to be found. Instead, on the dresser, a Mack-sized, long-sleeved T-shirt, sweatpants, and socks had been left sometime after Jasper fell back to sleep last night. Not wanting to go searching for Mack, his clothes, or his tracking beacon while practically naked, Jasper pulled on the garments and chuckled when they swallowed him whole. He could think of a better way for that to happen, and it involved the handsome stranger who'd welcomed him into his home.

After rolling up the pant legs, tightening the drawstring as much as possible, and pushing the sleeves up to his elbows, Jasper remembered to transform his ears again before leaving the bedroom in search of his clothes and host. He found the latter by the stove in the kitchen, cooking something that smelled delicious. Mack heard him enter and eyed Jasper over his shoulder. He took a long look at the man wearing his two-sizes-too-big clothes, then grinned. "Good morning. How are you feeling?"

"Better, thank you. I appreciate everything you've done for me." When Mack turned back toward the stove, Jasper couldn't stop his gaze from dropping to the man's fine, denim-covered ass.

Holy stocking stuffers!

"Glad I was in the neighborhood and could help." Something in his tone put Jasper on high alert. The man was clearly curious about how Jasper ended up in the forest in the middle of a blizzard without transportation. But Mack's following words said he would hold off on the interrogation for a little longer, but no doubt, it was coming. "Are you hungry? I've got bacon, eggs, hash browns, and toast—it'll be ready in a few minutes. Grab some coffee if you want." He gestured toward a machine on the counter.

"Thanks. Breakfast sounds great, but you wouldn't happen to have any hot chocolate, would you?"

"I doubt it, but you can look in the pantry over there." He gestured toward it with the spatula in his hand. "If I have any, it's from one of those food baskets my sister sends every now and then."

Jasper opened the door Mack had indicated and searched the contents on several shelves. When he didn't find what he wanted, he glanced over his shoulder to ensure he wasn't being watched. Mack's attention was on the meal he was preparing, so Jasper rubbed his fingers together, and a box of his favorite hot chocolate appeared on a shelf. Smiling, he picked it up. "Found some."

Mack turned slightly, his eyes narrowing as he replied, "Really?"

"Yup. Guess I got lucky." He removed one of the packages. "I just need some hot milk and a mug."

A few minutes later, the two sat at the dining table with hot drinks and platefuls of food. Baxter was sacked out on the floor by Mack's feet. They ate silently for a bit before Mack posed the first of what would probably be about a dozen questions. "So, Jasper Sugarplum, are you from around here?"

He swallowed a bit of bacon. "Um, no, I'm just passing through. I live further north."

"Hmm." Mack evidently wasn't happy with the vague response but didn't ask how far north. "So, what were you doing in the middle of nowhere during a blizzard?"

"It wasn't snowing when I started my trek, but then I got lost and disoriented when it got worse." Okay, that was close to the truth. While elves weren't supposed to lie, they could stretch the truth quite a bit in order to maintain a cover when walking among the human population.

"You picked a hell of a time to go on a nature hike. This storm isn't supposed to let up until tonight, and another one is coming right behind it. The landline is down, and I can't get cell service. The roads are blocked, too, so you're stuck here for a few days."

"Well, I'm sorry for the inconvenience, but thank you again for rescuing me and your hospitality."

"You're welcome."

Silence descended once again, but it didn't last very long. Mack sipped his coffee, then asked, "So, what do you do for a living?"

That was an easy question since it was part of his training. "I'm in quality assurance for a toy company. We have several factories around the globe, so I travel a lot."

"A toy company. Hmm." There was that tone of skepticism again.

"Yes, a toy company. And you? What do you do for a living?"

"Me? I'm an author."

Jasper's eyes widened. "Really? I've never met an author before. What do you write?"

"Serial killers, mainly. You know, ones that bury dead bodies in forests, so they'll never be found."

He had no idea what to say to that, but it reminded him that he was all alone with this stranger, and no one knew where he was. While he always tried to look for the good in humans, he wasn't naïve to think there weren't evil ones out there. He felt the blood drain from his face. "Uh—"

The corners of Mack's mouth ticked upward, and he let out a booming laugh. "You should see your face. I'm just kidding. Not about being an author, but I write science fiction novels."

Relief coursed through Jasper's veins, and he chuckled. "Okay, got me on that one."

"Sorry, but it was too easy a setup not to mess with you for a bit."

When both their plates were empty, Jasper stood

and picked them up. "Since you cooked, it's only right that I clean."

Mack raised an eyebrow at him. "I'm not the type of person who usually turns down an offer to have my dishes washed, but are you sure you're up to it?"

"Absolutely. I feel much better this morning. The medication and sleep did wonders." *And so did the fact that I'm an elf.* But, of course, he couldn't say that.

"Okay then. Thank you. We have some power with the generator, so you can watch TV if you want. The satellite's out at the moment, but I have dozens of movies you can watch on Blu-ray. Or, if you're into reading, feel free to grab something out of that book-case over there." He gestured to a large display next to the living room fireplace.

"Are any of your books there? I'd love to read one." And that was true. This man intrigued him more than anyone had in a very long time, and Jasper wanted to get to know him better, even if it was only in a round-about way.

Mack got to his feet and grabbed a few things from the table before following Jasper into the kitchen. "Yeah, top shelf. If you don't mind, I'm going to write for a few hours. I don't want to put extra exertion on the genera-tor, so I'll use my old typewriter. It might get a little loud."

"No worries."

While Mack poured himself another cup of coffee, Jasper washed the dishes and pans in the sink. An odd feeling of domesticity overcame him, but he forced it aside. "Oh, by the way, where are my clothes?"

"Hanging in the laundry room at the end of the hall. They were still damp this morning, but you can wear what you have on until they dry."

Jasper glanced over his shoulder to see Mack staring at his ass. When the man's gaze lifted and slammed into Jasper's, there was heat in his eyes before Mack quickly turned away. "I've got work to do."

And now, Jasper was even more intrigued by his rescuer. Was the man gay? He appeared to be. Was Jasper going to explore that? He knew he shouldn't, but, holy peppermint, did he want to.

After cleaning the kitchen, Jasper wandered down the hall to the laundry room. He cursed under his breath when he spotted the tear in his jacket where his tracking beacon should have been. It looked like he would be stuck there until his telepathy came back online, and he wasn't sure if that was a good or bad thing.

Seven

Mack pounded away on the old-fashioned typewriter at his desk in the corner of the great room. He tried to keep his mind and gaze from focusing on the man curled up on his couch in front of the fireplace, reading Mack's first book. At the rate Jasper turned the pages, it appeared he was a speed reader. Mack's mother had been the same way. She often read full-length novels in a single day—her library card was well-used.

It felt odd yet strangely comforting to have someone else in his house for the first time since he moved in. Up until today, Mack never felt isolated. Lonely, yes, because the one person he wanted to share the house with was gone. But, as for lack of visitors, it never bothered him before. He had his writing, Baxter, a TV, books, and a computer to keep him company. The occasional phone calls from his editor, publisher, agent, and siblings, on top of a once-a-month trip into town, gave him the minimal human contact essential not to go insane. He hadn't wanted or needed more than that. However, having Jasper in his house, even for less than a day, had Mack coming out of his shell for a bit.

He actually teased Jasper at breakfast, something Mack hadn't done with anyone in years. And it felt so good to laugh—he was surprised he remembered how. He also noted the way the other man had eyed his torso and ass as if he were interested in seeing them up close and naked. Mack had done the same thing to his guest, but Jasper wouldn't be there long. Once the snow eased up and the roads were finally cleared, the guy would be on his way back . . . north?

No, it hadn't escaped Mack's notice that the man was vague in a few of his answers, but it wasn't his place to push for answers, although his curiosity was getting the better of him. On top of all that, he couldn't deny his attraction toward Jasper. Suddenly, his dick was coming back to life for someone who wasn't Michael—and that thought had a touch of anger and grief rearing their ugly heads for a moment. Mack didn't want to be drawn to anyone other than the love of his life—the love he'd lost. With that in mind, Mack forced himself to reread what he had already written over the past hour in order to get his concentration back on the task at hand.

Three hours later, Mack had barely added another

word to the story he was working on. He was too in tune with the man who'd invaded his space. That was how he tried to refer to Jasper in his head, to remind himself he didn't want to have anyone else in his home, but it became more difficult to convince himself as the day went by. Surprisingly, Jasper had been very quiet, seemingly content to read for hours. Even when he got up to use the bathroom or grab something from the kitchen, he barely made any noise, so that wasn't what had distracted Mack. Nope, that was because of the man himself. Something about Jasper was just . . . different. And it intrigued Mack more than he was willing to admit.

Twice since Mack started writing that morning, Jasper silently refilled Mack's coffee cup and let Baxter out to do his business. The man seemed so comfortable in his unfamiliar surroundings that he didn't ask what needed to be done. He just did it. Part of Mack liked that, while the rest of him didn't want Jasper getting too comfortable in his private refuge.

Unable to focus on his word count, Mack stood and stretched his arms over his head. He immediately felt Jasper's gaze on him, dragging up from his feet to the tips of his fingers. Fighting an avalanche of feelings, especially lust, Mack decided to try to get to know the current object of his unwanted obsession—since they were stuck together with no separation in sight for another few days.

Picking up the fresh coffee Jasper had given him a

few moments before, Mack strode over to the fireplace, set the mug on the mantel, then picked up two logs and added them to the roaring blaze. "Do you have family that's going to miss you tomorrow?"

Jasper let the book he was reading drop to his lap and tilted his head. "Tomorrow?"

"Yeah, you know, for Thanksgiving?"

For the past few hours, Jasper was happy to sit on Mack's couch and read the incredible book the man had written. He was about three-quarters of the way through the 562-page novel, not only because he was a fast reader but because the story had drawn him in and refused to let go. The words touched him as if the man himself ran his fingers over Jasper's skin. Mack was a very talented author, and when he got home, Jasper would have to make sure they had his books in the North Pole Community Library for others to enjoy.

Home. For the first time in his life, Jasper felt at home in a place that wasn't at the top of the world. The chalet was cozy and inviting, but its owner caused Jasper to feel like he belonged there, which was odd since he barely knew Mack.

One thing was obvious to him now, though—Mack was definitely gay. A photo of him passionately kissing another man sat on one of the bookshelves. Several other photos of the couple were on an end table and the mantel, and Jasper wondered who the unknown man was and where he was now. Since Mack had asked personal questions, maybe Jasper could get a few in of his own.

"My family knows I travel a lot, and if I can make it for dinner tomorrow, I will. If I can't, they won't worry." At least, he hoped not. Having an elf go entirely off the radar didn't occur often. In fact, it'd been over a hundred years since the last time it happened if Jasper's recall was correct. "What about you? Were you planning to join your significant other for the holiday?"

When a surprised look crossed Mack's face, Jasper gestured toward the mantel. "I noticed the photos of you two."

Mack frowned as he turned his attention back to the fire. "No. He's dead."

Those dreadful words sounded even worse when accompanied by Mack's flat tone, and Jasper couldn't help himself. Dropping the book on the couch, he got to his feet and crossed over to Mack, embracing him without a second thought. "I'm so sorry for your loss. I didn't know."

Mack sucked in a startled breath and stood stiffly for a few moments, but then his arms lifted and wrapped around Jasper's torso. The difference in size between the two men was never more apparent than at that moment, and desire rushed through Jasper's body. When he felt Mack's hardening cock against his belly, he knew what he felt wasn't a one-sided attraction.

When Mack tried to pull away, Jasper tightened his hold. He wasn't ready to let the man go just yet and was relieved when Mack's body relaxed again. One of Mack's hands cupped the back of Jasper's head and grasped a lock of hair before tugging it until Jasper looked up into his face. A storm, more powerful than the one outside the house, raged in Mack's eyes. His gaze dropped to Jasper's mouth, and he dipped his head down, bringing their lips only an inch apart. His deep voice rumbled, vibrating from his chest. "Tell me to stop right now, and I will, but if you don't say anything, I'll take what I want."

Instead of giving a verbal response, Jasper rubbed his erection against Mack's hip and tilted his chin up, inviting the man to do whatever he wanted.

Eight

Throwing caution to the wind, Mack growled and then smashed his mouth against Jasper's. He licked and nibbled on the other man's lips until they parted and allowed him entry. Mack rubbed his tongue along Jasper's, reveling in the sweet taste he found there, probably from the hot chocolate he'd been drinking all day.

With his cock throbbing in his jeans, Mack cupped Jasper's ass and lifted him until their groins ground together. *Holy hell.* Mack would come like a randy teenager if he didn't slow things down a bit.

It was so unlike him. Mack never had sex with a stranger before in his life, but that's where things were headed. He couldn't stop himself. It didn't mean anything—he knew that. It was months since he last jacked off and just under three years since he'd had sex. What he felt was nothing more than an animalistic need to mate. To blow off steam. To have human contact in the most primal way.

Jasper's hands ran up Mack's chest to his shoulders and then to his nape. Mack ripped his mouth from the delicious one it'd devoured and kissed along Jasper's jawline to his ear. "I've never done this before—with someone I barely know, I mean. But, damn it, I want you."

"I want you, too, Mack. Please!"

Grabbing the hem of Jasper's oversized shirt, Mack drew the garment up his body and over his head before tossing it aside. His own shirt quickly followed, and then he attacked his prey once more. Their tongues danced a sensual tango as their hands explored each other's bodies. Jasper was smaller than Mack, and while Mack's chest had a moderate amount of dark hair that trailed downward, Jasper's was almost bare. There was only a smattering of fine blond hair, but nothing hid his rosy nipples, and Mack couldn't wait to get his mouth on them.

He took two handfuls of luscious ass cheeks and lifted Jasper again. "Put your legs around me."

When his order was followed, he hungrily indulged in kissing the man as he carried him into his bedroom, kicking the door closed behind them. The last thing he wanted was for Baxter to join them, thinking this was some kind of new game.

Dropping Jasper unceremoniously on the bed, Mack didn't waste any time getting the man naked. He untied the string holding the borrowed sweatpants up and yanked the garment down, exposing a very nice cock and set of balls. Mack licked his lips as he stared at the incredible male specimen laid out like a feast for him. Jasper reached down and tugged on his stiff shaft. "Please, Mack. Don't make me beg."

He smirked as he undid the snap and zipper of his jeans. "Oh, you'll beg all right." He froze. "Shit, I forgot about your back and head. I didn't hurt you, did I?"

Jasper shook his head. "I barely felt a thing other than how hard you made me."

Relieved, Mack let his gaze wander down to the other man's prominent erection. Oh, yeah. Jasper was totally into what was happening here. After he was buck naked, Mack climbed onto the bed, grasped Jasper's wrists, and pinned them above the man's head. He rubbed his cock against Jasper's, groaning as the friction urged him to fuck like there was no tomorrow. Their hips gyrated in time as if they'd done this before. Mack stared into Jasper's eyes—they were the color of the sky when there wasn't a cloud in sight. "Damn, you're so freaking sexy."

"I was just thinking the same thing about you. I love that you're bigger than me. It makes me want to surrender."

"Surrender, huh?" Mack punched his hips forward, imitating what he wanted to do to Jasper's mouth and ass. "I like that."

He nuzzled Jasper's neck and worked his way down

to the nipples he was dying to taste. He alternated, sucking and laving the tiny buds, causing Jasper to squirm under the ministrations. "Oh, yes! Oh, fiddlesticks!"

Mack chuckled. "Fiddlesticks? That's a new one for me during sex."

He ground his pelvis into Jasper's, pre-cum oozing from both their slits, making them sticky—not that either minded. Mack returned to Jasper's mouth, plunging his tongue inside. Reaching down, he wrapped a hand around both their cocks and smiled when Jasper gasped and then begged, "Oh, Mack! Please! Harder! Squeeze harder."

He was more than happy to comply with such a request. Together, they fucked Mack's fist, panting and moaning as they climbed to the pinnacle of ecstasy. Mack would've given anything right then for a condom and some lube, but those weren't on his shopping list of essentials over the past few years.

Biting Jasper's bottom lip, Mack increased the pace of his bucking hips. A tingling started in his spine as his balls pulled up into his body, preparing for him to detonate. His orgasm rushed to the surface, but he wanted to take Jasper over the edge with him. Bringing his mouth to the other man's ear, he said, "Come for me."

That was apparently all Jasper needed because he bellowed with his release as he ejaculated all over his abdomen and Mack's hand. Seconds later, Mack exploded, and his cum mixed with Jasper's. The pleasure coursing through Mack's body short-circuited his brain, and it took a few moments for it to come back online.

Gasping for air, Mack rested on his forearms, keeping the majority of his weight off Jasper as he sagged against the mattress, completely spent. When Mack was confident his legs would hold him up, he stood and strode into the en suite bath. After cleaning himself, he returned to the bed in a post-coital haze and washed Jasper's abdomen and chest with a damp washcloth.

While this was probably a one-and-done experience, Mack wasn't willing to let the encounter end just yet. He tossed the washcloth through the open bathroom door onto the tiled floor and then climbed back onto the mattress. After all that exertion and the best orgasm he'd experienced in almost three years, he needed a nap. Apparently, so did Jasper because he seemed to have trouble keeping his eyes open as he studied Mack's face.

Mack stretched out next to Jasper. "Turn onto your side." When he did, Mack snuggled close to Jasper's back and fell asleep within seconds.

Nine

That was the most incredible orgasm in Jasper's entire life. Considering he was over three centuries old, that said a lot. He slept for about an hour after Mack crawled in behind him and wrapped a muscular arm around his torso. While Jasper was wide awake now, Mack was still asleep, a light snore coming from him, and Jasper didn't want to disturb him. Well, he did, and he didn't. Not waking Mack meant staying cocooned in his warm embrace. But rousing him might result in another round of phenomenal sex.

Hmm. This or that?

He wiggled his ass against Mack's groin, and the man stirred. The hand covering the left side of Jasper's chest squeezed before trailing down to where his cock already stood at full attention. Mack's own erection nestled between Jasper's ass cheeks. A sleepy voice murmured in his ear. "I wish we had some condoms and lube."

His hand clasped around Jasper's straining shaft as he rocked his hips forward.

Jasper moaned with need and rubbed his fingers together. "There's some in my jacket."

"Really?" The sleep was instantly gone from his voice.

Turning his head, Jasper glanced over his shoulder. The items hadn't been in his jacket a few seconds ago, but they were there now. Being an elf with magical powers came in handy at times.

Mack pushed up from the mattress, his eyes glittering with delight, but then his brow furrowed as he frowned. "What the—? What's with your ears? They're pointy again." His gaze shifted. "What the fuck? Your back! The bruises are almost gone. How—?"

Not finishing that question, he leaped from the bed and stared at Jasper in shock. "What in the hell is going on? Who are you?"

Well, fruitless fruitcake.

He screwed up. In Mack's presence, Jasper couldn't think straight. Between the fantastic sex and the relaxing nap, the magic that transformed his ears had ebbed, leaving them natural—or what was natural for him.

He should cast a spell and make Mack forget everything that'd happened in the past twenty-four hours, but he couldn't bring himself to do it. He wanted him to remember how good they were together in bed because Jasper would never forget it. So, he did what he never thought he'd do with someone who wasn't from the North Pole—he told the truth about himself. "I'm an elf—one of Santa's elves, to be precise."

Grabbing his jeans and shirt and yanking them on, Mack snorted. "Yeah, right. And I'm the Abominable Snowman."

Jasper sighed. It wasn't that he expected Mack to give credence to the fact he was face-to-face with a real elf right away, but it still sucked that he didn't. Getting to his feet, Jasper picked up his clothes and got dressed. "Actually, the Abominable Snowman really is a myth. Look, I know it sounds unbelievable, but it's true. Santa does exist, and so do his elves."

"I thought elves were short." The sarcasm was hard to miss. He still thought Jasper was pulling his leg.

"Well, that's one of the things most people are misinformed about. Just like humans, we come in all shapes and sizes. "

Shaking his head, Mack jerked open the bedroom door and stormed out to the living room with Jasper on his heels. Baxter rushed over to Mack, whining as he looked up at Jasper. The elf gave the dog a small smile. "It's okay, Baxter. Your master is having difficulty believing in what he thinks is unbelievable."

"You're talking to my dog now?"

Jasper shrugged. "I just answered the question he asked."

"What?" Mack began to pace, running his hands through his hair. "I'm going insane. That's what's happening. I've been isolated for too long, and now I'm going nuts."

"You're not going nuts."

Before Jasper could say anything more, in his head he heard, "Mission Control to Agent Sugarplum, do you copy? Come in, Agent Sugarplum."

While Mack tried to convince himself he was going crazy, Jasper kept his mouth shut and responded to NPMC via telepathy. "This is Agent Sugarplum—I hear you, Mission Control."

"Hot cider! I've got him, Santa!"

Cheers erupted in the background, and then the next voice Jasper heard was the big boss himself. "Ho, ho, ho, Jazz! Glad we finally got ahold of you. Are you okay?"

Was he? Physically, he was back in prime condition, but emotionally? He felt like his heart was being ripped from his chest. Somehow, he'd fallen for a complete stranger—a human to boot—and in less than twenty-four hours! How the heck had that happened? And on top of everything else, he would have to report to Santa that he told Mack who he really was. Maybe he could hold off on that for a little while.

"I'm fine, sir. Just banged up a bit, but I'm almost completely healed. Did Nip make it back okay?"

"He did. From what the elves at the stables told me, he searched for you until he realized the storm was too severe and he needed help. He then made it back here in record time to let us know you were missing. We've been trying to locate your tracking beacon or get through to you ever since."

Eyeing Mack, who babbled about hallucinations, a straightjacket, and a rubber room, Jasper sighed inwardly. "I lost my beacon in the fall and bumped my head, which is probably why you couldn't reach me."

"Are you safe where you are?"

"Yes, sir. I'm sheltered at home with a human and his dog. The blizzard over Montana might make it too dangerous for a team to come get me just yet." That was putting it mildly. "But I'll be fine until it passes."

He hoped so because there seemed to be a new storm about to rage *inside* the chalet.

"Very good. Keep Mission Control posted, and we'll send a team as soon as possible. Santa out."

Ten

*T*his guy's a fruitcake, Mack thought to himself as he paced in front of the fireplace. *Well, if he's a fruitcake, then how do you explain the pointy ears and the bruises that should've been visible for at least a week and are practically gone now? Huh? Yeah, how do you explain all that? You're going insane, that's how. None of this is real. You're sleeping and hallucinating about everything that's happened since the storm started. Right?*

Stopping short, he pinched his arm—hard. And, sure enough, it hurt like hell.

Okay, so you're not dreaming. That means it's time for a straightjacket and a rubber room. Wonderful.

"Mack?"

After taking a deep breath and letting it out slowly, Mack turned to face Jasper . . . the fucking Christmas elf. "Yeah?"

"You can pinch yourself all you want—it won't change the fact that I'm real."

"Elves don't exist."

Jasper flopped onto the couch next to Baxter, who'd climbed up there at some point in the last few minutes. "Says who?"

Mack lifted an eyebrow. "Uh, anyone with a brain."

"Why, because they've never seen one before? You write science fiction. I'd think you'd be more open to believing that some myths could be real."

"My books are fiction—as in make-believe. They're not based on reality." He started pacing again and tried to recall if insanity had run in his family. His sister might know—she did a lot of research for their family tree a few years ago.

"Most fiction and many myths *are* based on kernels of reality, at the very least. Take your character Orion, for example." He picked up the book he'd tossed onto the couch earlier. "This is a very good story, by the way. But my point is that Orion is an ancestor of Dracula, who was based on a real person—Vlad the Impaler, right? A vile man, according to my grandfather. He avoided crossing paths with that one as much as possible."

Coming to a halt in front of Jasper, Mack put his hands on his hips and stared at him. Jasper's ears were as pointy as ever at the moment. "Crossing paths? You do realize Vlad the Impaler lived and died over six hundred years ago."

"Mm-hmm. Elfin lifespans are much longer than our human counterparts."

"Of course they are." He rolled his eyes and began to turn away but then paused. "So, how old are you?"

"Three hundred and twenty—that's about thirty-two in human years."

"In human—" Mack ran a hand down his face. *What in the actual fuck?* He stood there, having a conversation—after just having sex with—a guy who claimed to be a 320-year-old elf.

Glancing out the window, he saw the snow still falling at a fast clip. He couldn't get rid of Jasper any time soon—and did he really want to? Okay, so the guy was weird—like fairy tale weird, but he didn't look or act like a serial killer.

Wait a minute!

Unable to help himself, Mack burst out laughing. "I get it. This whole thing is a joke to get back at me for the serial killer thing this morning."

"No, it's not." Jasper sighed. "What can I do to convince you I'm an elf?"

A snort escaped him. "Uh, a miracle might work. Or is that out of your realm?"

Standing, Jasper glanced around. He rubbed his hands together, then waved one with a flourish. Instantly, the decor of the living room changed. A huge Christmas tree stood in a corner, lit with multicolored lights, dozens of ornaments, and a shining star. Green garland with poinsettia flowers hung from the mantle.

Above that was a pine wreath adorned with a red bow. A Nativity scene and an array of gifts wrapped in pretty paper were tucked under the tree on top of a colorful quilted skirt. A massive gingerbread house sat on the dining room table. Candles, snowmen, reindeer and sleighs, Santa figurines, stockings, candy canes, ribbons, and bows were festooned around the room. Everywhere Mack looked, there were holiday decorations—it was like being in one of those all-things-Christmas stores. Or the home he once shared with Michael.

Fuck!

He didn't know what was going on, but he sure as hell didn't like it. Mack took a threatening step toward Jasper and growled. "I don't know how you just did that, but make it go away. Now!"

Jasper appeared startled at the anger in Mack's words but showed no signs of fear. With a snap of his fingers, the room returned to normal—stark and joyless. Without another word, Mack stormed to his bedroom and slammed the door behind him.

Eleven

An hour later, while Mack brooded in his room, Jasper wandered into the kitchen and found most of what he needed to make his mother's famous goulash. What was missing quickly and quietly appeared with a twitch of his hand. It would keep him busy and was the least he could do for Mack after everything that happened over the last twenty-four hours.

As he mixed the ingredients, he contacted Mission Control—grateful he could communicate with the North Pole again. One of his best friends, a female elf named Daisy, answered him. "Oh, Jazz, I was so glad to hear you're okay! What can I help you with?"

After Mack's blow-up, Jasper did a little snooping around the house. Thanks to Baxter's help, he found Michael's last name and birthday in a book Mack had given him as a present. Armed with that information,

Jasper decided to do some research on the man who'd meant so much to Mack. Baxter was only a puppy when Michael died, so he didn't remember all the details about the man who gifted him to Mack as a surprise one day.

"I need you to look up a Michael Sherman—deceased." He rattled off the birthday, an approximate age based on the photos in the living room, a description of Michael, and that he'd lived in the lower half of Montana.

"Oh, I found him! That was easy enough. Let's see what I can tell you." She gave him some basic facts, but nothing that would help him until she said, "According to the records, he was a true believer in Christmas. He loved the holiday and spreading joy. Sadly, he was killed in an accident on Christmas Eve."

So that's why Mack freaked out. Not because the decorations had simply appeared but because they were Christmas decorations.

"Thanks, Daisy."

"You're welcome. Stay safe, and I'll see you soon."

Jasper stirred the cooking goulash in the stock pot and glanced down at Baxter, who'd joined him. "Think we can convince your human that Michael would be upset if he knew Mack hated Christmas now?"

"I'm not sure, but I'll try to help," the dog responded.

While the goulash simmered and Mack sulked,

Jasper and Baxter devised a plan to help Mack believe in Christmas again.

After locking himself in his bedroom, Mack laid down atop the rumpled covers of his bed and did something he hadn't done in a long time. He cried his eyes out. But as he did, the oddest feeling came over him. He sensed his anger and grief pouring out of him with each tear that fell. It was a cleansing of sorts.

It occurred to him he'd never cried like that since Michael died—oh, he'd shed many tears, but never a soul-purging weeping that seemed to ease one's pain.

As his sobs eventually ebbed, an emotional exhaustion swept over him.

Closing his eyes, he felt himself drift as he conjured up an image of Michael, and not unexpectedly, the man appeared surrounded by Christmas decorations. This wouldn't be the first time Mack spoke to his deceased lover in his mind, but it'd been a while.

"So, you slept with a Christmas elf, huh?" Michael asked with a chuckle. "I don't know why you're so shocked. I used to tell you stories about them all the time. Hmm, I wonder. Since he's a gay elf, does that make him a fairy? You'll need to ask him that for me."

Mack couldn't help but smile. Both of them had been secure in their homosexuality long before they ever met, but Michael had been the queen of gay jokes, often throwing them out at the oddest of times, not caring who he might offend. If anyone had an issue with Michael being gay, that just brought out the jester in him, which resulted in his "flaming fairy" side, as he called it, to emerge. That man could strut his stuff like a runway model when he got going.

"I miss you, Michael."

"I miss you too, but I'm tired of watching you mope. That's why I sent Jasper your way. I figured you needed a sexy but fun distraction."

"You sent him my way? Why?"

"Because jealousy doesn't exist here, and you need to start living again, my love. Yes, I'm gone. But it's wonderful here, and someday you'll join me, but until then, I want you to be happy, not just going through the motions of existing. I was delirious to discover so many things we thought were myths were actually real, and one of those is Santa Claus and his elves. You know how much I love Christmas, so I sorta nudged Jasper in your direction. I knew he couldn't get seriously injured, so I hope he'll forgive me for the bumpy ride. It's not every day an elf falls out of his sleigh while flying over Montana."

"Did you say flying?"

"Yup—ask him about it. And believe what he tells you, Mack. Believe in Christmas and all its magic again because it's real."

Twelve

Mack woke up with a start, and his gaze searched the room—a room that still had the faint aroma of sex hanging in the air. It was dark outside, but the wind still battered the chalet. He had no idea what time it was. His cell phone was in the great room next to his typewriter, and he'd never bothered getting an alarm clock for the bedroom. He usually woke up when he felt like it and went to bed the same way.

Sitting up, he ran a hand down his face and mulled over everything that happened earlier. Not only what happened in his bed, but also the fact Jasper claimed to be an elf and then Michael appeared in a dream to tell him Jasper was the real deal.

Many myths are based on kernels of reality.

Okay, so maybe Jasper had a point. Heck, look at all the people who believed in one God or another. They never saw one in person, but it never swayed their faith that they existed. Who was Mack to say differently?

Staring at his closed bedroom door, Mack let out a slow breath, then climbed out of bed. He strode into the bathroom, washed his face, and then stared at his reflection in the mirror. The stubble on his jaw that he'd shaved off two days ago was full again. He usually let it grow for about a week or two before pulling out the razor. He contemplated shaving for a moment but realized he was just stalling. He needed to leave his room and see what Jasper was up to. Baxter had to be fed too.

Before he could change his mind, Mack walked through the bedroom and opened the door to the great room. The aroma of something cooking filled his nose, and his stomach growled with hunger. On his way to the kitchen, he inspected his surroundings. After his "conversation" with Michael, Mack felt a twinge of disappointment that not a single Christmas ornament or light could be found.

When he entered the kitchen, he stopped short and felt the corners of his mouth pull up into a grin. Standing in the middle of the room, Jasper danced with Baxter. The big dog was up on his hind legs, with his paws on Jasper's shoulders, as the two did what looked to be a box step. Jasper smiled when he spotted Mack, then let go of Baxter, who dropped onto all fours. "Hey, we were just dancing."

"I see that. No music, though."

He ruffled Baxter's head. "Oh, it's there—you just have to know how to listen for it. I made goulash for dinner. Are you hungry?"

Mack nodded, grateful Jasper wasn't holding his earlier tantrum against him. "Yeah, I am. I fell asleep for a while. What time is it?"

"A little after nine." Jasper grabbed a clean bowl from a cabinet and filled it with a ladleful of the contents of the stockpot. "Baxter and I already ate, but there's plenty for you. Go sit at the table, and I'll bring it to you."

Fifteen minutes later, Mack had eaten his fill of the best goulash ever. Jasper had also made fresh bread and warmed it enough to melt the butter Mack slathered over it. "That was delicious. Thank you."

The grin that spread across Jasper's face at the compliment penetrated Mack's heart. "You're welcome." He picked up Mack's bowl and bread plate. "While I clean this up, why don't you add a few more logs to the fire, and we can sit and watch a movie."

Mack's brow furrowed. He had a feeling he was being set up. "What movie?"

"One of my favorites. *Miracle on 34th Street*. The original, although they're all good."

"Sorry, but I don't have that one in my collection."

Jasper chuckled. "That's okay. I do."

That morning, Mack might've thought that was an odd statement, but now, after seeing the trick Jasper did with the Christmas decorations, he knew better than to question him. After putting more logs on the fire and stoking the flames, he took a seat on the couch as Jasper carried two steaming mugs from the kitchen. He handed one to Mack as he sat beside him. "No coffee for you tonight. This is hot chocolate and peppermint schnapps—my favorite. It's called a peppermint Patty."

Mack took a sip, and the delicious chocolate and mint flavor hit his tongue. "Mm. That's good."

"Told ya." Jasper snapped his fingers, and the TV came on. Another snap had the introduction to *Miracle on 34th Street* rolling across the screen. This version had been Michael's favorite too—with a young Natalie Wood playing the girl who didn't believe in Santa Claus.

Picking up the remote, Mack lowered the volume and shifted to face Jasper. The elf . . . damn, that was weird . . . looked at him expectantly. "You have questions."

"A ton of them."

Jasper took a sip of his drink. "Okay, shoot."

Mack didn't know where to begin, but his mind flittered toward what happened in his bedroom earlier. "Are elves like humans? I mean, we had sex, so you have to be at least a little human, right?"

"Elves are mostly human. We evolved the same way but veered off in a slightly different direction somewhere along the line. Magical powers became part of our genetic makeup in the twelfth or thirteenth century. We learned about it in history class in school, but honestly, I had a crush on the teacher, so I don't remember all the details. I was too busy drooling over him, and that was over two hundred and fifty years ago. So, sue me if I can't explain it better than that."

Mack laughed. "Okay. So, do you really live at the North Pole?"

"Yup. There's a whole city up there, but thanks to our advanced technology, the rest of the world doesn't know it exists. Next question." He was clearly enjoying this.

"What were you doing in Montana?"

"Well, I'm an agent for the Department of Naughty and Nice Affairs. It's my job to observe, evaluate, and report back on children to ensure they're on the correct list in time for Santa to check it once and then check it twice."

"Seriously? What happens if they end up on the naughty list?"

"Truthfully, it's very rare for that to happen. By the time Christmas Eve rolls around, Santa pretty much gives everyone a pardon with hopes they'll do better next year. What can I say? He's an old softie."

"You said you're over three hundred years old. How old is . . . jeez, I can't believe I'm asking these questions. How old is Santa?"

"The big guy is over seventeen hundred years old and doesn't look a day over a thousand."

Another bubble of laughter spilled from Mack's

mouth. The whole conversation was so surreal. Reaching out, he ran his fingers over the point of Jasper's right ear. "How do you make these disappear?"

Jasper touched the tops of both ears, and they rounded out. "A little magic. They'll revert back when I sleep or have sex."

Mack's eyebrows shot up. "That's, uh . . . interesting."

Taking a deep breath, Jasper grasped Mack's hand. "Please don't get upset, but I contacted North Pole Mission Control and asked about your Michael." When Mack's smile dropped, and he tried to pull his hand away, Jasper tightened his grip. "I'm sorry, but I wanted to know why you had such a devastating reaction to the decorations before. If I'd known he died on Christmas Eve, I would've done something else to prove to you I was an elf. I truly am sorry."

His shoulders sagging, Mack shook his head. "It wasn't your fault. In fact, I dreamed of Michael while I was napping. He told me he sent you my way."

"He did?"

"Said to tell you he was sorry for tossing you out of the sleigh. Were you really flying?"

It was Jasper's turn to burst out laughing. "Yes, I was, and it doesn't surprise me that Michael caused me to end up in the forest. Those who have gone into the afterlife tend to twist fate to their own liking when it comes to comforting their loved ones. Honestly, it was the first time I ever had an accident like that. Nip might be a little traumatized over it, but I'm good."

"Nip?"

"The substitute reindeer who was pulling my sleigh during the storm. My regular navigator, Digger, hurt himself playing reindeer games."

"Of course he did. This is—"

"Weird."

Mack took another sip of his peppermint Patty. "That's putting it mildly."

"So, what else did Michael tell you."

Tilting his head, Mack pursed his lips. "That it was time for me to move on. Time for me to believe in and enjoy Christmas again."

"Do you believe in love at first sight?"

His eyes widened at the change of questioning. "Um, yeah. It was like that for me and Michael. The second I saw him approaching my table for the blind date we were set up on, I knew he was someone special."

Jasper cupped Mack's jaw. "That's kind of what happened to me when I saw you sitting in the chair in the spare bedroom, watching over me."

Thirteen

Jasper couldn't believe he blurted that out, but it was true. He realized it while cooking earlier. He'd never had such a visceral reaction to another being before—elf or human. But when it came to Mack, Jasper was in love. He didn't want to leave the man behind when the rescue team came for him, but he knew he couldn't stay. That left only one other option, but first, he had to clear it with Santa before he proposed the idea to Mack. And there was no way to guarantee either would allow it to happen.

All his thoughts fled when Mack leaned forward and brushed their lips together. "This is absolutely crazy. I've only felt like this once before in my life, and that was with Michael. But all I have to do is look into your beautiful eyes, and I feel . . . love. How can that be after only knowing you for a day? What am I supposed to tell my family? I'm in love with an elf? They'll have me committed. And where do we go from here? You obviously have to return home. What happens then?"

"I don't know just yet. What I do know is I want to make love to you—right here, right now. Please."

A smile spread across Mack's face. "You mentioned something about condoms and lube earlier?"

Jasper jutted his chin toward the coffee table, where a box and a small bottle appeared. Mack chuckled, brought Jasper's hand to his mouth, and kissed his palm. "I think I like those magical powers of yours."

"They come in handy." Jasper got to his feet and stripped his clothing off. Mack watched and cupped his growing erection. Straddling Mack's thighs, Jasper kissed the other man with all the passion he felt. Growling, Mack grasped Jasper's ass and moved so quickly that Jasper didn't know what happened until he was on his back, pinned to the cushions. He wrapped his legs around Mack's hips and lifted his pelvis, letting their hard-ons drag against each other.

Pushing up on one hand, Mack reached back, grabbed a handful of his shirt, and pulled it over his head. Kissing his way down Jasper's body, he worshiped each inch of skin with his mouth, teeth, and tongue. Quivering with desire and anticipation, Jasper begged. "More, please, Mack. More!"

Mack licked Jasper's navel as the elf's cock bumped his chin. Scooting further down, Mack lifted his gaze to Jasper's as his mouth engulfed the erection he hovered over. Jasper's hips bucked as wet heat surrounded him, and Mack took him to the back of his throat. When he swallowed around the tip, Jasper whimpered. He hung on by a thread, not wanting to climax and have it over too soon.

While licking and sucking on the cock in his mouth, Mack cupped Jasper's balls, rolling and squeezing them gently with a loose fist. Jasper writhed with pleasure, reaching down and running his fingers through Mack's thick hair. When the man hummed in delight, Jasper gasped at the delicious sensations it evoked.

Putting his hands on the backs of Jasper's thighs, Mack pushed until his knees hit his chest. Mack released the cock he'd been savoring and lifted his head, eying Jasper's rear hole that was now exposed. "Such a pretty asshole. I can't wait to get my dick inside you and fuck you like you've never been fucked before."

"Oh, figgy pudding! Yes!"

Mack chuckled. "I get a kick out of how you curse."

Releasing Jasper, Mack stood and removed his pants, revealing the beautiful, hard cock Jasper wanted to feel break him in two. Reaching over to the coffee table, Mack grabbed a condom and the lube. As Jasper watched, licking his lips and palming his own hard-on, Mack rolled on a condom, then knelt between the elf's thighs. "I don't want to hurt you."

"Trust me, you won't." Hooking his hands under his knees, he opened himself for Mack. "Please hurry."

Mack growled, then poured some lubricant on his

fingers and stiff cock before tossing the bottle aside. As he used one hand to spread the slick liquid over his shaft, Mack ran the fingers of his other hand over Jasper's puckered hole. Jasper moaned. "Oh, please, don't make me wait any longer. Fill me! Take me!"

Applying pressure with his index finger, Mack entered Jasper's ass, and the elf saw stars. He panted and watched as Mack fucked him with one and then two fingers. "Oh, yes! More!"

Mack scissored his fingers, stretching and lubricating his passage. His gaze remained on where his digits disappeared into Jasper's body. "Damn, so fucking pretty. Clench for me. Oh, yeah, like that! Again."

Groaning, Mack pulled his fingers out and lined his cock up. He started to ease his way in, but Jasper was impatient. He wrapped his legs around Mack's hips and used his feet to push him forward. Mack thrust inside hard and fast until he was balls deep. They both froze, waiting a moment for Jasper's body to relax against the massive invasion and not to come the second either moved again.

Finally, back in control, Mack slid almost the whole way out, then plunged deep again. That time, the tip of his cock rubbed on Jasper's prostate, eliciting a gasp followed by a moan and more begging. He couldn't help himself. Having Mack in him, fucking him, felt incredible. "Oh, Mack, harder. Faster. Please."

Mack picked up the pace, becoming relentless in his

assault. Jasper wanted everything this man could give him. Mack's balls slapped against Jasper's ass as he pounded into him.

Grasping his own cock, Jasper masturbated in time to Mack's thrusts. He climbed to the top of the world and knew when Mack took him over the edge, it would be an experience unlike anything he'd ever known.

A tingling began in Jasper's spine, and when Mack shifted slightly, changing the angle of his hips, Jasper detonated, shooting his cum over his abdomen and chest. His ass clamped down on Mack's cock, and the man stiffened and let out a bear-like roar as his orgasm ripped through him. His face reddened with the combination of exertion and pleasure.

Covered in sweat, Mack collapsed atop Jasper, who gladly took the man's weight. As they lay there, gasping for air and reveling in the bliss they found in each other's arms, Jasper knew he'd been ruined for anyone else but Mack. The man was his perfect match—his destiny—and no matter what, he'd find a way for them to be together.

Fourteen

Thanksgiving morning, they awoke to the sun shining through the slats of the window blinds. It was well after 11:00, which wasn't surprising since they had stayed up half the night talking and making love. Neither one had wanted to fall asleep, and Jasper wasn't sure when they finally surrendered to exhaustion.

With a brief check-in with NPMC, Jasper learned the second storm had turned north and would completely miss Blunt. To say he was disappointed was an understatement. That meant a rescue team would come for him as soon as he could give them the coordinates.

With Baxter leading the way, Jasper and Mack used snowshoes to trek back to where the human and dog found the elf two days earlier. It took a little digging on Baxter's part, but they were able to find Jasper's tracking beacon. Once they returned to the chalet and turned the device on, Mission Control picked up the signal and relayed the longitude and latitude to the rescue team. Mack and Jasper had an estimated forty-five minutes in real-world time to say goodbye, but Jasper hoped it wouldn't be forever. With any luck, Santa would grant him an early Christmas wish and let him return with an offer he prayed Mack wouldn't refuse.

Jasper cuddled into Mack's side as they sat on the couch with steaming mugs of hot chocolate. Baxter sat on the floor with his big head in the elf's lap while Mack put his arm around Jasper's shoulders and sighed. "What's going to happen after your team picks you up? Is it like something out of *Men in Black* where you flip a switch, and I forget the last two days?"

Jasper let out a sad laugh. "The North Pole was in an uproar over that movie. It hit a little too close to home with some of the technology."

"So, I'll have no memory of you?"

"I don't know. That's how it's supposed to go, but I've been thinking there might be a way around it. I have to talk to Santa first, but I'll make sure that your memory won't be erased until I do. I'll be back as soon as possible, and we'll talk if that's okay."

Mack kissed Jasper's temple tenderly. "That's more than okay. I don't know which is harder—remembering someone you love after they're gone or knowing you won't remember them at all."

Jasper sat up and stared at Mack. "Did you just say you loved me in a roundabout way?"

"*Harrumph.* I guess I did. I don't understand how, but I was a goner from the moment you told me your name. I fought it—I mean, who falls for someone that quickly? But I'm going to miss you."

"I'll be back, I promise."

"But you can't stay here."

He shook his head. "As much as I want to, no." He tried to lighten the mood. "But when I *do* come back, will you let me decorate the place for Christmas?"

Mack chuckled softly. "Yeah, I just might."

Before either of them could say anything else, NPMC contacted Jasper. "Mission Control to Agent Sugarplum, your transport is waiting outside your location."

Not wanting to leave but knowing he had to, Jasper placed a chaste kiss on Mack's cheek. "They're here. Walk me out?"

"Of course."

Standing, he petted Baxter's head. "You, too, Taliesin the Snow Hunter."

"Who?" Mack asked.

"That's Baxter's real name. It's okay, though. He likes the name you gave him too."

He shook his head. "As weird as this all is, it's really kinda cool that you can talk to my dog."

After pulling on their coats, Mack walked out the front door, hand in hand with Jasper and Baxter on their heels. But the human stopped short when he saw the sleigh and reindeer parked in his front yard. Jasper smiled at Mack's slack jaw and wide eyes. The red and gold sleigh was big enough to fit the two-elf rescue team that came for him, with room for several more. Since it was just a pickup at this point, there hadn't been a need for an entire squad. Tethered to the front of the sleigh were three reindeer—Clyde, Dexter, and Sven.

Jasper squeezed Mack's hand and got his attention. "I have to go."

Sadness filled Mack's eyes. "I know. But you'll be able to come back for a visit, right?"

"As soon as I can. I promise." Jasper closed the distance between them and put his arms around Mack's neck. The kiss they shared was passionate and tortured, but one Jasper would savor for the rest of his life.

Reluctantly, they separated, and Jasper licked his upper lip. "I'll see you soon. I love you."

Mack swallowed hard and just nodded, clearly on the verge of crying. Jasper knew precisely how he felt.

Walking backward toward the sleigh, Jasper stored the vision of Mack standing there in the snow in his mind so he could recall it later. Even if Mack had to have his memory erased, Jasper would never forget.

When he reached the sleigh, he turned around and climbed in, shaking hands with the other elves. Once he was seated, the pilot snapped the reins. "On Clyde, on Dexter, on Sven!"

The sleigh slid forward, and within seconds, it lifted off into the air. Jasper laughed at the stunned expression on Mack's face and waved at him. As they gained altitude, he settled in for the trip and prepared to make his case to Santa.

Mack was miserable. Jasper had left three days ago, and Mack still hadn't heard from him. His heart was broken for the second time in his life. What had he done to make the Fates cause him so much pain?

After Jasper left Thanksgiving morning, the chalet regained power and the internet. Mack had foregone the football games in favor of a satellite channel that ran a full day of the greatest Christmas movies of all time. Some were comedies, like *Christmas Vacation*, while others were heartfelt, such as *It's a Wonderful Life*. Yesterday, he binged on the sappy Hallmark Channel holiday movies. Today, ever since he woke up, he'd watched Christmas cartoons and stop-motion animation films, including his old favorites—*Frosty the Snowman, Rudolph the Red-Nosed Reindeer, and Merry Christmas, Charlie Brown.*

Mack hadn't written a single word in days. Instead, he researched everything he could about Santa Claus and his elves during commercial breaks. While most of it was speculation and folklore, as Jasper had said, there were kernels of truth buried under all that fluff.

Picking up his mug of hot chocolate—there seemed to be an endless supply of it in the pantry now—he carried it out to the great room and sat down at his computer. He was about to continue his research when Taliesin—yes, he changed Baxter's name—barked loudly and ran to the front door. Mack rushed over, hoping beyond hope Jasper had returned.

He flung open the door, and his chin almost hit the floor. No, it wasn't Jasper standing there, but a large, robust man dressed in a red suit with white trim, a matching hat, white gloves, and black boots. A white beard and mustache covered his jaw and upper lip. With a twinkle in his eyes, something about him screamed to Mack that this was the real Santa Claus and not someone simply dressed as him. He was shorter than Mack thought he'd be—around five feet seven.

In the front yard behind the man was a sleigh, similar to the one that came for Jasper the other day, but it only had two reindeer on leads. Mack's eyes widened when he noticed their names were stitched in black lettering onto a wide portion of their red harnesses—Blitzen and Comet. *Holy cow!*

The jolly old elf held out his hand, drawing Mack's attention back to him. "*Ho, ho, ho.* You must be Mack Wynters. I'm Kris Kringle, and I've heard a lot about you."

While Mack shook Santa's hand, he struggled to say something—anything. But all that came out of his mouth was, "Uh . . . um . . . ah . . ."

"Do you mind if I come in for a bit? I want to talk to you about something."

"Uh . . . um . . . sure! Yes, yes! So sorry." He stepped to the side of the door and opened it wider. "Please, please come in."

Santa strolled inside, stopping momentarily to pet the St. Bernard, who stared adoringly at him. "Well, hello there, Taliesin the Snow Hunter. It's a pleasure to meet you too."

The dog lifted a paw, and Santa shook it, then pulled something out of his pocket. "I have something special for you, Taliesin." He held up a medal hanging from a red, white, and green ribbon. "It's the North Pole Canine Medal of Honor for your heroic rescue of Agent Sugarplum."

The dog let out a resounding woof as the ribbon was placed around his neck. Santa chuckled. "Just doing your job? I think you went above and beyond the call of duty that day, my friend, and I'm forever in your debt."

Mack gaped as the legendary *Santa Claus* conversed with his dog.

Unbelievable! No, scratch that. Michael, you were right! I totally believe.

Finally gathering his wits and remembering his manners, Mack gestured toward the couch and recliners. "Please, have a seat. Can I get you anything to drink?"

"No, thank you. The missus made sure I had a full thermos of hot cocoa for the trip." The big man sat on one of the recliners as Mack lowered himself onto the couch. Taliesin jumped onto the cushion beside him, proudly showing off the gold medal, in the shape of a snowflake, hanging from his neck.

Tilting his head, Santa studied Mack. "You're probably wondering what I'm doing here."

"Uh, yes. That's definitely high on my list of questions right now."

Santa smiled. "And I'm sure that list is quite long. Let me see if I can answer as many as possible. First, I've come to express my undying gratitude to you for aiding Agent Sugarplum—Jasper—and offering him your hospitality."

"It was my pleasure."

"So I heard." He laughed when Mack's cheeks burned. "I'm just teasing. The thing is, Jazz broke several rules during his time here with you." When Mack opened his mouth to defend Jasper, Santa held up his hand. "However, when he came to me and explained that he'd fallen in love with you, I didn't have the heart to punish him. He's a darn good elf—one of my best. But he's been moping around since returning to the North Pole. I don't want to lose him, but I may have to."

Mack's brow furrowed. "Why? You can't fire him, can you?"

"No. I've never fired an elf, and I'm not about to start with Jazz. But he did give me an ultimatum. Allow him to become human or grant you semi-immortality—meaning, transform you into an elf."

His eyes grew wide. "What? You—you can do that? Either of those things?"

"Yes, my boy, I can. I never have before, but I do possess that power. I received a full dossier on you yesterday. I'm sorry for your loss of Michael. While I have many powers, the births and deaths of humans are things I can't control. Another is human nature. I can offer hope and joy, but if someone's not willing to accept either of those things, I can't do anything to change it.

"Your grief caused you to lose your beliefs for a time, but they aren't gone forever. You just needed a reason to believe again. I think that came in the form of Jazz. You made a list this morning of everything you needed to get during a shopping trip. If I'm not mistaken, a Christmas tree, ornaments, and lights are at the top of that list."

Mack was dumbfounded—more than he was a few minutes ago. He *had* made a list and planned to go into town tomorrow to get everything on it. He wanted to decorate for the holiday for the first time in years.

"Anyway," Santa continued. "I'm here to offer you one of two things. For Jazz to return to you fully human, or for you to come with me to the North Pole as my newest elf.

"Now, before you decide, I must explain a few things. If you choose for Jazz to become human, he'll be subject to all the diseases and perils of being one. I cannot guarantee a long life for him or you. However, if you choose to become an elf, you'll have an exceptionally long life ahead of you—and Taliesin is welcome to join you." The St. Bernard's tail thumped against the couch. "You'll outlive your siblings, their children, and even their great-great grandchildren. You'll live at the North Pole but will be able to temporarily transform yourself to blend in with humans again and visit your family—who miss you very much, by the way. They'll continue to believe you're who you are right now, and you'll never be able to tell them otherwise. The decision is all yours. Once you've made up your mind, Jazz will make his own choice. Just know that either way, he's determined to choose you."

Gaping, Mack had no idea what to say about everything Santa had just told him. His mind whirled like a tornado.

Getting to his feet, Santa adjusted the thick black belt under his round belly. "You don't have to decide now, but you must do it soon. You have until the year's end." He snapped his fingers, and a snow globe appeared on the coffee table in front of Mack. "After you make your decision, rub the globe, and I'll know to visit again. Just don't do it on Christmas Eve since that's a busy night for me, you know."

Mack picked up the globe as he stood. "There's nothing in here but snow."

"At the moment, yes. When you decide your destiny, you'll see it there. In the meantime, let me help you with your decorations." He waved his arm in a grand, sweeping gesture, and the great room was transformed into a Christmas wonderland, just as Jasper had done a few days ago, complete with a decorated tree. This time, though, Mack looked at everything with awe instead of grief and anger.

"Well, I best be going. I've got lots of work to do, and you have a lot of thinking to do." Santa held out his hand, which Mack shook. "I'll talk to you soon, Mack."

In the blink of an eye, Santa was gone. Rushing over to the window, Mack found the reindeer and sleigh had disappeared too. He turned and inspected the beautiful Douglas fir with all its lights and decorations. Front and center was a gold ornament—Michael's family heirloom. For the first time in years, Mack felt joy in his heart and reveled in it.

Fifteen

New Year's Eve . . .

Jasper sighed as he pulled on the jacket of his silver tuxedo over a white button-down shirt. He really didn't want to go to the New Year's Eve party at Father Time's, but his friends warned him that they would come and drag his ass there if he didn't show up on his own. A few elves had offered to set him up with a date, but he turned them all down. Going out with someone else didn't feel right when his heart was in Montana.

Santa still hadn't told Jasper his decision yet. Yes, giving the big guy an ultimatum was risky, but Mack was worth it. Unfortunately, Santa had refused to make a ruling until after the New Year. Knowing his boss, Jasper hadn't pushed for an answer yet, but as of tomorrow, all bets were off. If Mack couldn't come to him, Jasper would go to Mack. He'd wanted to return to help Mack decorate for Christmas, but Santa forbade it, saying it was too busy for him to let anyone take time off.

Checking himself in the mirror, Jasper determined he looked as good as he would get. He just wished he felt as sparkly as his suit.

A knock sounded at the door, and Jasper figured it was Daisy. She'd offered to ride over to the party with him. Striding across his apartment's living room, he opened the door, and his knees nearly buckled. Standing before him, with Taliesin at his side, was Mack, wearing a black tuxedo and a huge smile. "Hey there, stranger. I heard you needed a date for New Year's."

When Jasper stood there, frozen, Mack stepped forward. "Are you going to just gape at me or invite us in?"

Jasper's mouth watered as he stared at the handsome man he was in love with. The last thing he ever expected was for Mack to show up at the North Pole. "How? What—what are you doing here? How are you here?"

"Santa made me an offer I couldn't refuse."

He pointed at his ears, and Jasper's eyes grew wide. "You're—you're an elf! Holy stocking stuffers!"

Leaping forward, Jasper threw his arms around Mack's neck and kissed him as if it was years and not weeks since he last had his mouth on the other man's . . . er . . . elf's.

When they finally came up for air, Jasper stepped back and eyed Mack. "You look gorgeous. I'm going to be the envy of every elf there tonight." He cupped Mack's jaw. "Are you sure about this? Did Santa—"

"He explained everything and gave me a few weeks to think about it. Before I made my final decision, though, I'd contacted him through a snow globe he gave me—that was really cool, by the way. I had a bunch of questions he needed to answer—one of them being what my job would be up here. He said I could continue to write books on one condition."

Jasper tilted his head. "What's that?"

"Apparently, he wants me to write his authorized biography. Said it might take a few hundred years, but it seems I've got all the time in the world now. The only problem is, I don't have a place to live. You wouldn't happen to know any sexy, blond-haired, blue-eyed elves who might have room in their bed for a big guy like me and his St. Bernard, do you?"

Grinning, Jasper grasped Mack's lapels, pulled him closer, and brushed their lips together. "I have just the elf in mind."

I hope you enjoyed Mack and Jasper's novella. Next,

check out my MM novella series next with *Scout: Cock & Bull Book 1.*

check out my MM novella series next with *Scout: Cock & Bull Book 1.*

Other Books by Samantha Cole

**Denotes titles/series that are only available on select digital sites. Paperbacks and audiobooks are available on most book sites.

TRIDENT SECURITY SERIES

Leather & Lace

His Angel

Waiting For Him

Not Negotiable: A Novella

Topping The Alpha

Watching From the Shadows

Whiskey Tribute: A Novella

Tickle His Fancy

No Way in Hell: A Steel Corp/Trident Security Crossover (co-authored with J.B. Havens)

Absolving His Sins

Option Number Three: A Novella

Salvaging His Soul

Trident Security Field Manual

Torn In Half: A Novella

HEELS, RHYMES, & NURSERY CRIMES SERIES

Don't Fight It

Don't Shoot the Messenger

Cock & Bull Series

Scout

Rico

Malone Brothers Series

Her Secret

Her Sleuth

Largo Ridge Series

Cold Feet

Antelope Rock Series
(Co-authored with J.B. Havens)

Wannabe in Wyoming

Wistful in Wyoming

Award-Winning Standalone Books

The Road to Solace

Scattered Moments in Time: A Collection of Short Stories & More

Standalone Books

Sweet Revenge (A Novella)

The Sugarplum Fairy (A Novella)

***The Bid on Love Series

About Samantha Cole

USA Today Bestselling Author and Award-Winning Author Samantha Cole is a retired policewoman and former paramedic. Using her life experiences and training, she strives to find the perfect mix of suspense and romance for her readers to enjoy.

Awards:

Wannabe in Wyoming (co-authored by J.B. Havens) won the bronze medal in the 2021 Readers' Favorite Awards in the General Romance category.

Scattered Moments in Time, won the gold medal in the 2020 Readers' Favorite Awards in the Fiction Anthology category.

The Road to Solace (formerly *The Friar*), won the silver medal in the 2017 Readers' Favorite Awards in the Contemporary Romance category.

Samantha has over thirty-five books published throughout several different series as well as a few standalone novels. A full list can be found on her website.

Sexy Six-Pack's Sirens Group on Facebook
Website: www.samanthacoleauthor.com
Newsletter: www.geni.us/SCNews

facebook.com/SamanthaColeAuthor
instagram.com/samanthacoleauthor
bookbub.com/profile/samantha-a-cole
goodreads.com/SamanthaCole
amazon.com/Samantha-A-Cole/e/B00X53K3X8